D0753752

MAMA CAT has three kittens

Denise Fleming

SCHOLASTIC INC.
New York Toronto London Auckland Sydney
Mexico City New Delhi Hong Kong

Mama Cat has three kittens,

Fluffy, Skinny, and Boris.

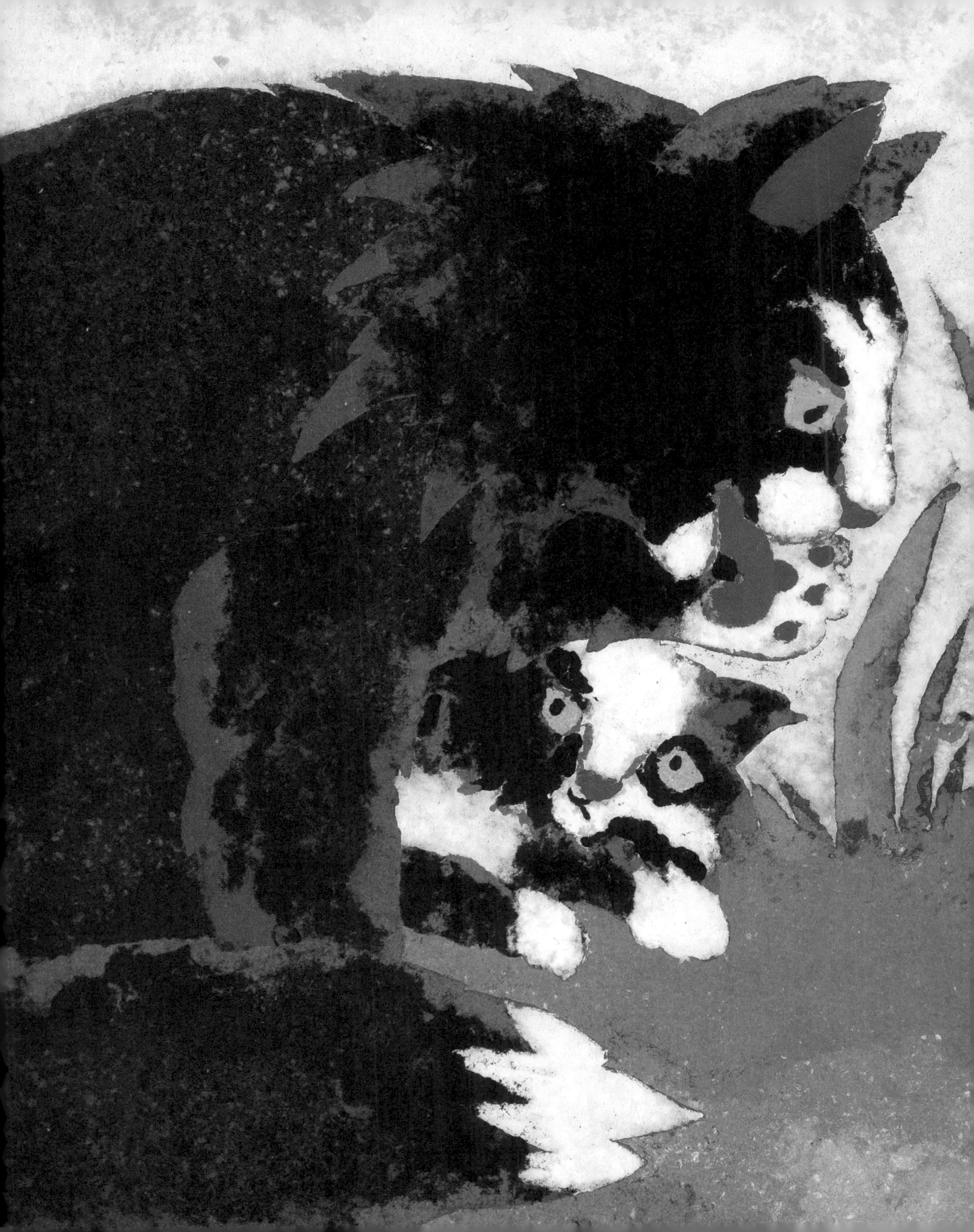

When Mama Cat
washes her paws,

Fluffy and Skinny
wash their paws.

Boris naps.

When Mama Cat walks
the stone wall,

Fluffy and Skinny walk
the stone wall.

Boris naps.

When Mama Cat sharpens her claws,

Fluffy and Skinny
sharpen their claws.
Boris naps.

When Mama Cat
chases leaves,

Fluffy and Skinny
chase leaves.

Boris naps.

When Mama Cat digs in the sand,

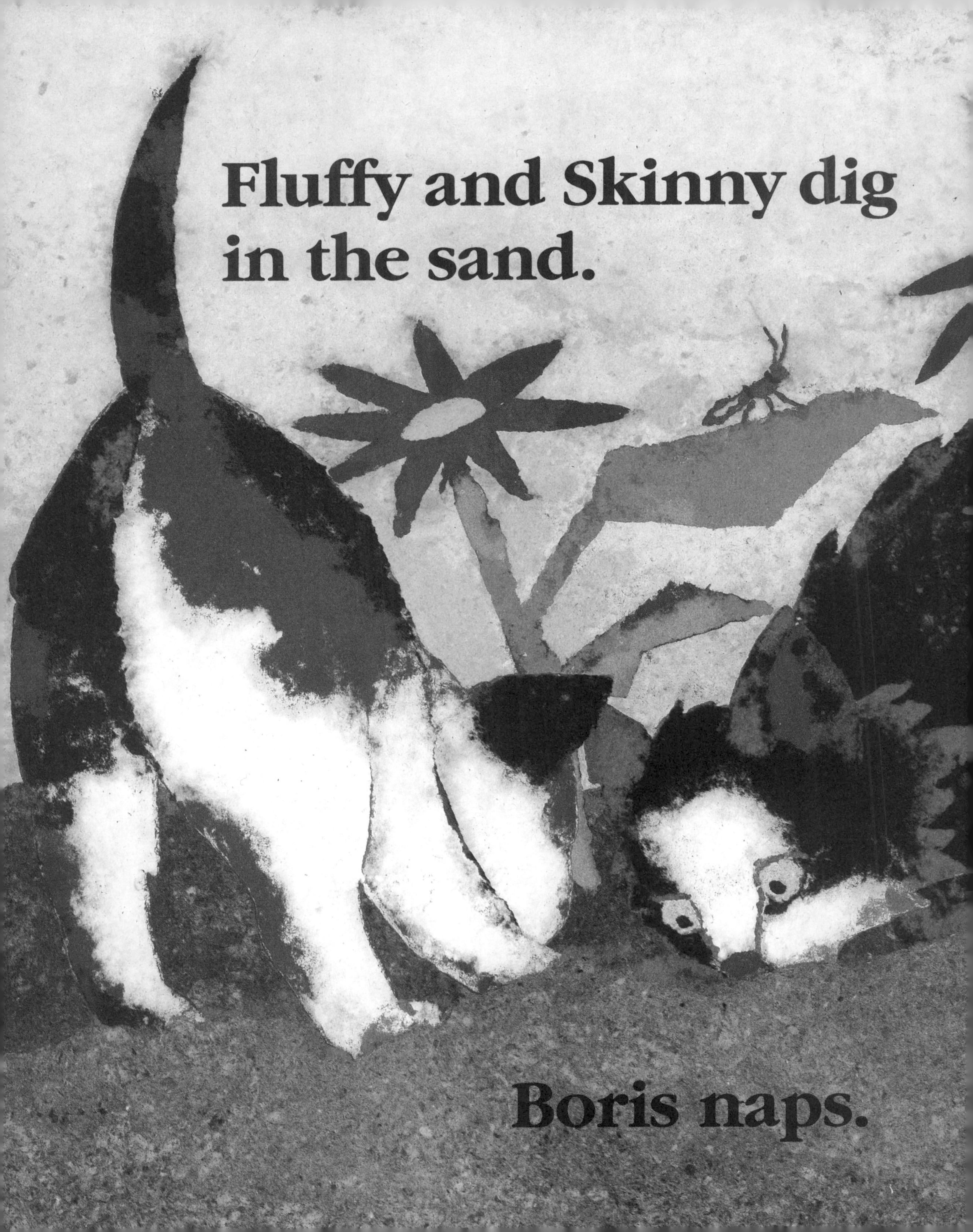

Fluffy and Skinny dig
in the sand.

Boris naps.

When Mama Cat
curls up to nap,
Fluffy and Skinny

curl up to nap.

Boris stretches,
yawns,

washes his paws,

and **pounces**

For Abigail, my first cat

No part of this publication may be reproduced in whole or in part, or stored in a retrieval system, or transmitted in any form or by any means, electronic, mechanical, photocopying, recording, or otherwise, without written permission of the publisher.
For information regarding permission, write to Henry Holt and Company, Inc., 115 West 18th Street, New York, NY 10011.

ISBN 0-439-06166-0

Copyright © 1998 by Denise Fleming.
All rights reserved.

Published by Scholastic Inc., 555 Broadway, New York, NY 10012, by arrangement with Henry Holt and Company, Inc.
SCHOLASTIC and associated logos are trademarks and/or registered trademarks of Scholastic Inc.

12 11 10 9 8 7 6 5 4 3 2 1 9/9 0 1 2 3 4/0

Printed in the U.S.A. 14

First Scholastic printing, October 1999

The artist used colored cotton rag fiber poured through hand-cut stencils to create the illustrations for this book.

on Fluffy, Skinny,
and Mama Cat.

Then Boris naps.